Room One,
First-Grade Friends

Mr. Scary   Junie B. Jones   Tattletale May   Herb

Lennie   José   Sheldon   Shirley

Lucille   Roger   Camille   Chenille

Laugh Out Loud with Junie B. Jones!

junie b. jones®

Jingle Bells, Batman Smells! (P.S. So Does May.)

by **BARBARA PARK**

illustrated by
Denise Brunkus

A STEPPING STONE BOOK™

Random House 🏠 New York

*To my dear Amy Berkower, whose patience and support
are so perfectly balanced by your utter good sense.
How lucky I am to have you as my agent . . .
and how grateful I am to have you as my friend.*

Text copyright © 2005 by Barbara Park
Cover art and interior illustrations copyright © 2005 by Denise Brunkus

Random House and the colophon are registered trademarks and A Stepping
Stone Book and the colophon are trademarks of Penguin Random House LLC.
Junie B. Jones is a registered trademark of Barbara Park, used under license.

JunieBJones.com

Educators and librarians, for a variety of teaching tools, visit us at
RHTeachersLibrarians.com

This title was originally cataloged by the Library of Congress as follows:
Park, Barbara.
Jingle bells, Batman smells! (P.S. so does May.) /
by Barbara Park ; illustrated by Denise Brunkus.
   p.   cm. — (Junie B. Jones series ; #25)
Summary: Junie B. Jones wishes that May would stop being such a
tattletale, but when she is stuck as May's Secret Santa it becomes real trouble.
ISBN 978-0-375-82808-9 (trade) — ISBN 978-0-375-92808-6 (lib. bdg.)
ISBN 978-0-375-82809-6 (pbk.) — ISBN 978-0-307-55714-8 (ebook)
[1. Talebearing—Fiction.   2. Gifts—Fiction.   3. School—Fiction.]
I. Brunkus, Denise, ill.   II. Title.
PZ7.P2197Jin 2005   [Fic]—dc22   2005008213

Printed in the United States of America   27 26 25 24 23 22 21 20 19 18 17 16

This book has been officially leveled by using the F&P Text Level Gradient™
Leveling System.

Contents

1
Peace and Goodwill

Dear first-grade journal,

Yay! Yay! Hurray!

Today is the last week before winter break!

Winter break is the school word for I gotta get out of this place, I tell you! 'Cause blabbermouth May is driving me crazy!

She is tattletaling on me
every day almost!

That's how come yesterday
I chased her down on the
playground. And I threw grass
on her head.

It was very fun. Except I
hope Santa did not see me do
that.

That guy watches me like a
hawk this time of year.

From,

Junie B., First Grader

P.S. Hey! Wait! I almost forgot!
Today all the first grades are
going to sing holiday songs

together! That will be a hoot, I
tell you because

Just then, I quick stopped writing. 'Cause I
couldn't believe my eyeballs!

That snoopy-head May was stretching
her neck across the aisle! And she was reading my journal page!

I slammed my book shut speedy fast.

"This is none of your beeswax, sister!" I
said.

But May was already jumping out of her
chair.

"Mr. Scary! Mr. Scary!" she hollered real
loud. "Junie Jones wrote a bad name about
me in her journal! She wrote that I am a
bladdermouth! And *bladder* is not a nice
word!"

I rolled my eyes at that dumb comment.

"It's not bla*dd*ermouth. It's bla*bb*er-mouth, May," I said. "*Blabbermouth* is spelled with *b*'s . . . not *d*'s."

Mr. Scary stood up at his desk.

"Girls . . . *please*," he said.

Then he was going to growl at us, prob-ably. But the phone rang from the office. And he had to answer it.

I crossed my arms at May. "*B* is the same letter that you always forget when you say my name, remember? And so maybe I should use *B* in a sentence for you."

I leaned close to her eardrum.

"Dear Bla*bb*ermouth May: My name is Junie *B.* Jones. How come you can't remem-ber *B*'s? Huh, May? Huh? Are you a *block-head* or something?"

May's face got very puffery.

Then, all of a sudden, she grabbed my

journal right off my desk. And she started
to rip out the page!

I tried to grab it back from her. But May would *not* let go of that thing! And so, me and her got into a tuggle.

I pulled real hard.

Then May pulled harder.

Then . . . *OOOMPHH!*

I pulled and pulled with all of my might! And me and my journal went flying back to my seat!

I hugged my book all safe and sound. But something did not feel right.

I looked down.

During the tuggle, May's sweater sleeve accidentally got hooked on my thumb.

And so, oh no!

Her sleeve got stretched across the aisle with me!

I quick untangled it from my thumb. But the sleeve did not bounce back.

Instead, it just stayed on my lap real longish and droopish.

I did a gulp at that thing.

Then—very slow—I looked over at May. And *kaboom!*

Her whole stack blew off!

She exploded out of her seat! And she hollered at the top of her lungs.

"MR. SCARY! MR. SCARY! JUNIE JONES WRECKED MY SWEATER SLEEVE! JUNIE JONES WRECKED MY SWEATER SLEEVE!"

Mr. Scary hung up the phone.

I quick wadded up May's sleeve. And I tried to give it back to her. But she would not even take it. And so, the sweater sleeve unrolled itself to the floor.

May's eyeballs popped out of her head.

"AAAAA! AAAAA! IT'S ALL THE

WAY TO THE FLOOR!" she yelled. "IT'S RUINED! IT'S RUINED! MY SWEATER IS RUINED!"

I tapped my fingers very thinking.

"Um . . . well, the whole sweater isn't ruined, actually. It's just that one sleeve, May," I said kind of quiet. "If you grow one arm to the ground, it will fit like a glove, probably."

May opened her mouth to holler again. But Mr. Scary was already hurrying down our row.

He did not say a word to us.

Instead, he took May and me by our hands. And he rushed us into the hall.

May's sweater sleeve dragged on the floor behind her.

She picked it up real limp.

"Look at this! Just look at it, Mr.

Scary!" she grouched. "Junie Jones wrecked my sweater! Junie Jones wrecks *everything*!"

I did a mad breath.

"I do not wreck everything," I said. "And anyway, this wasn't even my fault! *You're* the one who started it, May! *You're* the one who stoled my journal."

Mr. Scary looked down at me.

"*Stole,*" he said. "The word is *stole*, Junie B. Not *stoled*."

I sucked in my cheeks. 'Cause now was *not* the time for grammar.

"Fine. She *stole* my journal," I said. "She just grabbed it right off my desk. And she tried to rip a page out."

May kept on arguing.

"But I only took her journal because she wrote a bad name about me!" she said.

I stamped my foot.

"But May wouldn't even *know* about that name if she didn't snoop!" I said. "Snooping in someone's journal is an invasion of their piracy."

Mr. Scary did a little frown.

"*Privacy,*" he said. "It's an invasion of *privacy,* Junie B. Not *piracy.*"

I threw my head back. "For the love of Pete! Can't you just let it go? I'm trying to make a point here!" I said.

Mr. Scary glared his eyes. He said for me to *calm myself down, young lady.*

I jumped all the way in the air.

"I *AM* CALM!" I hollered back.

After that, I got marched speedy quick to the water fountain. And I had to drink some sips of water and settle myself.

I drank and settled.

Then I wiped off my mouth. And I rocked back and forth on my feet kind of nervous.

"Sorry," I said real quiet. "Sorry I got mad, Mr. Scary."

I looked up at him.

"Sometimes grammar makes my head explode," I said.

Mr. Scary smiled a little bit.

Then he took me back to May. And he talked to us in a calm voice.

"I really don't understand your behavior lately, girls," he said. "The holidays are the time of year when we try to spread peace and goodwill. But you two are treating each other worse and worse every day."

Me and May quick pointed at each other.

"It's *her* fault!" we shouted together.

Mr. Scary shook his head. "I don't care *whose* fault it is," he said. "If you two have another fight today, there will be no Holiday Sing-Along for either one of you. Instead, you'll be parking yourselves in the principal's office for the afternoon."

My body did a shiver at those words.

'Cause I've parked at Principal's before, that's why. And there's not a lot of singing that goes on down there.

"So what's it going to be, girls?" said my teacher. "Do you want to shake hands and make up? Or do you want to spend the afternoon at the office?"

My eyes glanced over at May.

She was standing still as a statue. And her eyes were staring at the floor.

I waited and waited for her to shake hands with me. But she did not look up.

Finally, Mr. Scary tapped his annoyed foot at us.

"Well?" he said again.

I waited some more.

But May still did not budge herself.

That's how come I did a big, loud breath. And I picked up May's long sweater sleeve. And I gave it a shake.

"There. Fine. I shaked with her," I said.

"*Shook,*" said Mr. Scary.

"Whatever," I said.

Then I dropped the sleeve back on the floor. And I kicked it over to May with my foot.

She did a gasp.

Then she quick picked it up and swatted the dirt off on my pants.

"Hey! Quit it!" I yelled.

Mr. Scary snapped his loud fingers at us.

May stopped swatting. "I was just get-ting the dust out," she said.

Mr. Scary filled his cheeks up with air. And he let it out real slow.

Then he took us by our hands again. And we walked back to Room One.

Peace and goodwill do not come easy.

2
Jingle Hats

The rest of the morning, we did arithmetic.

Arithmetic is the school word for adding and taking away. Only I couldn't even concentrate on my numbers that good. On account of May kept giving me mean looks. And flopping her sweater sleeve around.

Pretty soon, there was a knock on the door.

"COME IN, PLEASE!" said Room One.

Mr. Scary taught us to say that. Only I don't actually know why. 'Cause people come in anyway.

The door opened very slow.

And ha!

It was Mr. Toot, the music teacher!

He was carrying a big brown box in his arms.

It was dusty, I think. 'Cause when Mr. Toot plopped the box on the floor, Sheldon started to sneeze his head off.

Sheldon is very allergic to dust particles. Also, he is allergic to hoagies . . . and dairy products . . . and nature.

"AH . . . AH . . . AH . . . AHCHOO! AHCHOO! AHCHOO! AHCHOO!"

Mr. Scary looked at him real panicked. Then he quick picked up a tissue box. And he rushed to Sheldon's desk.

But Sheldon was already wiping his nose on his shirt sleeve.

"Ha! I beat you *again*, Mr. Scary!" he

16

said. "I beat you at that race every time I sneeze!"

Mr. Scary closed his eyes.

"I have told you before, Sheldon. We are not *racing,*" he said.

Sheldon laughed.

Then he threw his fist in the air. And he shouted, "SHELDON POTTS RULES!"

Mr. Scary rolled his eyes. Then he moved the dusty box farther away from Sheldon's desk. And Mr. Toot lifted the lid.

I stood up to look.

And wowie wow wow!

Guess what was in there?

ELF CLOTHES! That's what!

There were little green elf hats with jingle bells on their ends! Plus also, there were cute elf vests with belts!

Mr. Toot held them up for us to see.

"Boys and girls, our PTO made these costumes several years ago for our Holiday Sing-Alongs," he said. "Aren't they great? Every single first grader is going to get to wear one today!"

He started passing them out.

My richie friend Lucille got hers first.

She looked at it and made a face.

"Okay . . . Number one: I don't wear

this shade of green. And number two: I don't wear bell hats," she said.

Mr. Scary looked up at the ceiling.

Then he took Lucille by her hand.

And he walked her into the hall.

And she came back wearing her bell hat.

Pretty soon, all of the rest of Room One were wearing our bell hats, too.

We shook our heads.

The bells jangled very jingly.

"Hey! This room sounds just like a jingle-bell sleigh!" I said.

Mr. Toot did a chuckle.

"You're right, Junie B. Every year, one lucky class gets to wear the jingle-bell hats. And this year—because Room One has been so well behaved in music class—I chose you!"

All of the children clapped and cheered.

Except for not Lucille.

Instead, she threw her hands in the air and shouted, "What are the odds?"

After that, she flopped her head on her desk. And she didn't come up again.

Mr. Toot ignored her.

"And that's not *all* my good news, either," he said. "Because each year, the class with the bell hats goes onstage. And they lead the whole auditorium in singing 'Jingle Bells'!"

Room One jumped up from our seats.

"'Jingle Bells'! 'Jingle Bells'! Yay! Yay! We're going to lead 'Jingle Bells'!"

Mr. Toot smiled.

"Okay, everyone. Just to make sure that you know the words, we are going to have a short rehearsal!" he said.

"REHEARSAL!" we shouted. "YAY! YAY! REHEARSAL!"

Only too bad for us. 'Cause rehearsal was nothing to shout about.

We sang that dumb song a jillion times, I bet.

At first, it was kind of fun.

Only then it got real boring.

And so, that's how come I started singing funny different words.

They were funny words about Batman and Robin.

I sang them loud so my friends could hear.

Jingle bells,
Batman smells,
Robin laid an egg.
Batmobile
Lost its wheel,
And Joker got away.

Herbert and Lennie laughed and laughed.

May did a gasp.

Then she sprang up like a spring. And she started to tattle.

"Mr. Toot! Mr. Toot! Junie Jones is singing the wrong—"

I quick yanked her skirt.

"Psst! May! Are you *crazy*?" I whispered. "You and I can't fight anymore, remember that? If you tattletale on me, we'll be parking ourselves at Principal's."

May covered her mouth with her hands. And she sat down real fast.

"Oops. Never mind," she said to Mr. Toot.

I wiped my worried forehead.

"Whew. That was a close one," I said. "I saved our gooses."

May leaned across the aisle.

"*You* did not save our gooses, Junie Jones," she said. "*I* saved our gooses. *I'm* the one who didn't tattle."

She pointed her finger at me.

"But you better not sing those bad words at the Sing-Along," she said. "I mean it, Junie Jones. If you sing those bad words onstage, I will tell on you, *no matter what.*"

I did a big breath.

"*Robin laid an egg* is *not* bad words, May," I said. "An egg is nothing for a bird to be ashamed of."

"I don't care. It doesn't matter," she said. "You already ruined enough today, Junie Jones. You ruined my sweater. And you ruined my mood. But you're *not* going to ruin the Sing-Along, too."

She crossed her arms at me.

"Even if I get in trouble myself, I will *still* tell on you," she said. "You can count on that, Junie Jones."

After that, she leaned back in her chair. And she brushed her hands together real smuggy.

I looked and looked at that girl.

May is off her rocker, I believe.

3
Laughing All the Way

We went to the Sing-Along after lunch.

And ha!

The auditorium looked like Santa's workshop! There were a jillion cute elves in that place!

And wait till you hear this!

Room One got to sit in the very first row!

I sat in the seat right next to my friend Herbert.

"This Sing-Along is going to be fun! Right, Herb? Right? This Sing-Along is going to be the time of our life!"

Just then, May plopped down in the seat on the other side of me.

I stopped smiling.

"That seat is *saved*, May," I told her. "I am saving it for someone else."

She looked all around.

"For who?" she asked.

"For someone not you. That's who," I said.

May did not budge herself.

"You can't make me move, Junie Jones.

This seat is public property," she said.

She scooted closer to me. "I'm going to stick to you like glue. It's the only way to make you behave yourself today."

I showed her my teeth and I made a *grr* noise.

May did not look fearful.

Finally, I moved closer to Herb. And I pretended she was invisible.

Pretty soon, the Sing-Along got started.

Mr. Toot said to turn to page one in our holiday songbook.

The first song was "The Twelve Days of Christmas."

It is about a guy who gives his girlfriend a bunch of stupid presents.

I tapped on Herb real curious.

"What would you do with ten lords a-leaping, do you think?" I said.

He thought for a minute. "I'd take them back and get store credit," he said.

I nodded. That Herb has all the answers.

After that, we sang "Frosty the Snowman" and "Rudolph the Red-Nosed Reindeer" and "Winter Wonderland."

Finally, Mr. Toot stood up at his piano. And he said it is time for "Jingle Bells"!

Room One hurried to the stage.

It was very thrilling. Except for May kept on sticking to me like glue.

She stepped on my heels going up the steps.

Then she crowded in real close to me.

And she whispered in my ear.

"I'll be *listening* to you, Junie Jones," she said. "I'll be hearing every word you sing."

I smiled to just myself. 'Cause I had a surprise up my arm, that's why.

Pretty soon, Mr. Toot raised his hands to start the song.

I stood up straight and tall.

Then I took a big breath. And I sang the words out, loud and clear.

> Dashing through the snow
> In a one-horse open sleigh,
> O'er the fields we go,
> Laughing all the way. (ha, ha, ha)
> Bells on bobtail ring,
> Making spirits bright.
> What fun it is to ride and sing
> A sleighing song tonight!

My eyes glanced over at May.

Her face looked disappointed, almost.

I smiled. Then I took another breath. And I sang the chorus in her ear.

Ohhh . . .
Jingle bells,
Batman smells.
P.S. So does Maaay. . . .
I'd throw May
Right off the sleigh,
And then I'd drive away.

"HEY!" yelled May.

I laughed at that funny comment. 'Cause "HEY!" fit right into the song!

Room One sang the chorus again. But I was laughing too hard to sing.

It was the joke of my life, I tell you!

Only too bad for me.

'Cause—as soon as we got back to the room—May tattletaled her head off.

It was not good.

Mr. Scary called us up to his desk.

He said he is *very* disappointed in both of us. Only unfortunately there is not enough time left to send us to the office.

I started to relax a teensy bit.

Only just then, the *bad* news came.

'Cause . . . what do you know?

Mr. Scary said there was *exactly* enough time for him to write a note to our parents.

4
Going Last

Dear first-grade journal,

Mother and Daddy were not good sports about the note.

They said it is not funny to throw someone off a sleigh.

That made me laugh all over again.

I got sent to my room for a time-out.

Grown-ups do not understand
humor.
                From,
                Junie B., First Grader

I put down my pencil. And I glared my eyes at May's head.

She did not look up from her journal.

"I know you're staring at me, Junie Jones. But I don't care that we got notes sent home," she said. "My mother was *proud* of me, in fact. She said that you *deserved* to get tattled on."

I glared harder.

Sometimes if you glare hard enough, you can melt people's heads. I saw that on a movie commercial once.

It was PG-13, I believe.

I kept squinting and glaring. But May's head did not melt.

Finally, I rested my eyes.

I will try to melt her again at lunch.

Just then, Mr. Scary stood up at his desk. And he said to put our journals away.

"Boys and girls, today is the day for our first visit to the Holiday Gift Shop in the media center. Remember?" he said. "I sent a notice about it home to your parents last week."

He smiled. "Today we'll just be looking at the gifts," he said. "Then, on Friday, we'll go back with our money and buy the things we want."

I waved my hand all around.

"Guess what, Mr. Scary? Guess what? My mother said I get to spend one whole dollar on every person in my family! And that adds up to five entire dollars!" I said.

Lucille raised her hand.

"I can spend all the money in the world," she said. "I'm rich."

She stood up and fluffed herself. "My family has more money than you can shake a stick at."

Mr. Scary stared at her a real long time.

"Yes, well, fortunately, we don't need to be rich to shop at the gift shop, Lucille," he said at last. "Everything there is very affordable. Does everyone know what *affordable* means?"

"I do! I do!" I called out. "*Affordable* means *cheap*! My grampa Frank Miller *loves* cheap."

Sheldon jumped up. "Hey, my grampa loves cheap, too! My gramma calls him Cheap Old Ned."

Mr. Scary did a chuckle.

"Before we go to the gift shop, we're going to draw names for our Secret Santa gift party. That way, you'll be able to look for your Secret Santa gifts while you're down there, too," he said.

"We've been talking about this party all week. Can anyone tell me the most important rule about being a Secret Santa?"

Room One shouted the rule together.

"YOU MUST KEEP THE SECRET!"

Mr. Scary did a thumbs-up.

"Yes! Excellent! After you pick your name today, you *must* keep the name a secret," he said. "If you don't keep the secret . . . then you're not really a *Secret* Santa, are you?"

After that, he carried around a basket with everyone's names in it. And all of the children closed their eyes. And they picked a name.

Only too bad for me.

'Cause I am in the very last seat of the very last row.

And so—when Mr. Scary finally got to me—there was only one dumb name left in the whole entire basket!

And here is the dumbest part of all.

My teacher pretended I should be *happy* about it.

"Congratulations, Junie B. Jones!" he said. "You have the honor of choosing the final name!"

I drummed my fingers very annoyed.

"Okay, see . . . *one name left* is not actually called *choosing*," I said. "*One name left* is called *take it or leave it*."

I crossed my mad arms.

"I hate being in this seat, Mr. Scary. I hate it, I hate it! I get all the bad stuff back here," I said. "Even on the very first day of school, I got the only crayons that were already used."

Mr. Scary looked up at the ceiling.

"Yes, Junie B. I know that. We *all* know that," he said. "You mention it every time we color."

I looked at some of my friends.

"Did I mention that my red crayon wasn't even pointy? 'Cause it wasn't, you know. My red crayon was already—"

"*Roundy,*" said Lennie. "Yes. You told us that already."

I drummed my fingers some more.

"Did I mention that my greenie was broken in half?" I asked. "My greenie was just a teensy little—"

"*Stubbie*," said José. "Sí. You told us that, too."

Mr. Scary handed me the last name.

"Look. Right now, someone in this room is counting on you to be their Secret Santa, Junie B.," he said. "So you *really* need to read that name . . . *now.*"

I did a sigh.

Then I slid down in my chair real glum.

And I read the name.

5

Elf Ladies

My head clunked down on my desk real hard.

Mr. Scary read the name on my paper.

I raised up and looked at him. Then I clunked back down again.

Mr. Scary said to *please knock off the clunking.*

He took my hand and stood me up.

"Boys and girls, Junie B. needs a little bit of help reading the name," he said. "We'll be right back."

Then, quick as a wink, he hurried me

into the hall. And he closed the door.

I crossed my mad arms again.

"It's not fair, Mr. Scary. I *hate* that dumb name! I *hate* it. I *hate* it," I said.

My teacher snapped his fingers.

"You know I don't allow that word in my classroom, Junie B.," he said. "We do not *hate* in Room One."

I looked all around myself.

"But I'm not hating in Room One," I said. "I'm hating in the hall."

Mr. Scary looked at me.

"We don't hate in the hall, either," he said.

I raised my eyebrows real curious.

"Really? No kidding," I said. "A lot of children will be surprised to hear that."

Mr. Scary bent down next to me.

"Look. I know you and May aren't the best of friends," he said. "But this is the time of peace and goodwill, remember? And being a Secret Santa to someone you don't like is the truest form of goodwill there is."

I stared at him.

How do teachers come up with this stuff?

"*Really*, Junie B.," he said. "If you do something nice for May, you'll feel so proud inside. It will feel like a gift that you've given *yourself*."

I kept staring.

Maybe they pick it up at teacher school.

After that, he ruffled my hair. And he walked me back inside.

Pretty soon, all of the children lined up at the door. And we followed Mr. Scary to the gift shop.

The media center is down the hall and round the corner.

There was a gift-shop lady in an elf hat.

"Welcome, Room One!" she said. "Welcome to our Holiday Gift Shop!"

She smiled at us with big white teeth.

"I'm the president of the PTO," she said. "My name is Mrs. Hooks. But—just for today—you can call me Elf Ellen."

She looked all around. "Some of you might know my son, Jeff. Jeff is a big third grader."

Roger raised his hand in the air.

"I know Jeff Hooks," he said. "Jeff Hooks stole my milk money last year."

Elf Ellen stood there very frozen. Then she quick pointed across the room.

"Over there is Elf Wendy. Elf Wendy and I are here to help you with your gift selections. If you have any questions, please let us know."

Roger waved his hand again.

"Did Jeff Hooks ever get punished for what he did? I reported him to the office.

But I never got my money back."

Elf Ellen squinted her eyes at him. "I *meant* questions about the gift shop," she said.

After that, she passed out lists with all the gift items on them. And she told us about the prices.

"Children, as you can see, each of our five gift tables has a number on it," she said. "The number on the table matches the price of all the gifts on that particular table."

She pointed. "For example, all of the gifts on Table One sell for *one* dollar. And all of the gifts on Table Two sell for *two* dollars. And the gifts on Table Three sell for *three* dollars . . . and so on. Does everyone understand?"

Sheldon raised his hand.

"What about the gifts on Table Four?" he said. "How much do they go for?"

Elf Ellen sucked in her cheeks.

"Table Four has a *four* on it, doesn't it? *Four* means four. They sell for four dollars."

Sheldon nodded very thoughtful.

"I see," he said. "And Table Five?"

Elf Ellen looked at Mr. Scary. "Is he pulling my leg?"

Mr. Scary grinned.

Sheldon grinned, too.

Roger called out another question.

"Where's Table Thirty-five Cents?" he asked. "That's how much Jeff Hooks still owes me. Is there a Table Thirty-five Cents?"

Elf Ellen glared her eyes at Roger.

Then she quick reached into her pocket.

And she gave him thirty-five cents.

"There," she said. "Are you satisfied?"

After that, she took off her elf hat. And she put it on the counter. And she said she is going *on break*.

Roger smiled.

Mr. Scary smiled, too.

6
Giving

Elf Wendy clapped her hands together.

She said it is time for us to browse around. Except for please do not break the toys. And please do not eat the candy canes. And please do not blow our nose on the handkerchiefs.

I skipped to Table Two real excited.

'Cause I already saw something that I loved!

"Crayons! They got crayons!" I said very thrilled.

I picked them up and looked inside.

"Look! Look! The red has a sharp head! And greenie is not even a stubbie!"

I breathed their brand-new smell.

"Mmm. Mmm. Mmm. I would love, love, love to buy these things," I said.

Just then, my friend Herbert pulled me over to Table One.

"Tattoos! Tattoos! They've got tattoos, Junie B.! And they really, really look *real*," he said.

I did a gasp at those things.

There were pirate tattoos! And dragon tattoos! And dinosaur tattoos! And kitty-cat tattoos! Plus also, they had a nice variety of swamp animals!

"Whoa! That is all the tattoos a kid could ever dream of!" I said. "I would love, love, love to buy those things!"

Then, all of a sudden, my eyes glanced

over at Table Three. And my whole entire mouth fell open.

It was . . .

"GLOW-IN-THE-DARK BARRETTES!" I yelled real excited. "I've always, always wanted these things!"

"Cool," said Herb.

"I *know* they are cool, Herbert!" I said. "'Cause if you lose your hair in the dark, you will always, always be able to find it."

Just then, I felt a tap on my shoulder.

I spun around.

It was May.

"You shouldn't be wanting to buy gifts for *yourself*, Junie Jones," she said. "We are here to buy gifts for *others*."

I put my hands over my ears.

"WHOOPS! BAD NEWS! I CAN'T HEAR YOU!" I said.

May raised up her voice.

"It is nicer to give than to receive!" she shouted. "Giving is the spirit of the holiday season! I am a giver! I give, and I give, and I give, and I give!"

Just then, I thought I heard another voice.

I turned to look.

Mr. Scary was calling out some words to us, I think.

"YEAH, ONLY I CAN'T ACTUALLY HEAR YOU! I'VE GOT MY HANDS OVER MY EARS!" I called back.

He walked over to me and took my hands away.

His face did not look happy.

"You two aren't having another problem, are you?" he asked.

I shook my head very rapid.

"Nope. No sirree. No problem," I said. "I was just being thrilled at these gifts. That's all I was doing."

May stood up real proud.

"And *I* was just telling her to be a giver like me," she said. "My mother says that some people are born to be givers. And *other* people are born to be shellfish."

She glanced her eyes at me.

I stood there very puzzled.

Then I looked up at Mr. Scary.

"I don't even care for shellfish," I said.

He did a little smile.

He said May and I could browse some more. But to please keep our voices down.

Only what do you know?

As soon as he said that, we heard the loudest noise of the day!

And it's called *HA! SOMEONE IN*

ROOM ONE DID THE GIANTEST BURP IN THE WORLD!

Our heads spun around to see.

And we could not believe our eyeballs.

"LUCILLE! IT WAS LUCILLE!" we shouted.

Then all of us started laughing at once.

"LUCILLE BURPED! SHE BURPED! SHE BURPED!" we hollered again.

"I didn't even *know* rich people burped!" I said.

"Me neither!" said Sheldon. "I am pleasantly surprised."

Lucille stamped her expensive foot.

"BUT I DIDN'T BURP! I DIDN'T! I DIDN'T! I DIDN'T!" she yelled.

She held up a round toy in her hand. It looked like a beanbag, sort of.

"IT WAS *THIS* THING!" she said.

"*THIS* THING BURPED! NOT ME!"

Lucille gave it a squeeze.

And HA!

ANOTHER GIANT BURP!

Room One laughed until our sides hurt.

Even May was laughing!

Plus Mr. Scary was laughing, too!

A good burp can bring the whole world together, I tell you!

Mr. Scary went to Table Five.

And he read us some information about that toy.

"It costs five dollars. And it's called a Squeez-a-Burp," he said.

All of us clapped at that silly name.

"A Squeez-a-Burp! A Squeez-a-Burp!" we hollered. "Squeeze the Squeez-a-Burp again, Mr. Scary!"

Mr. Scary smiled. But he shook his head no. And he put it back on the table.

"I think we've had enough burping for one day. Don't you?" he said.

Room One did a groan.

"How can you have too much burping?" said José. "Burping is pure entertainment."

Sheldon nodded. "I agree. My grampa can burp the 'Star-Spangled Banner,'" he said. "I've been trying to bring him in for Show-and-Tell. But he's booked solid."

I looked at Sheldon very admiring.

He comes from a talented family, I think.

After that, all of the children hurried to Table Five. And we gathered around the Squeez-a-Burps.

We read the writing on one of the bags.

It said:

SQUEEZ-A-BURP
World's Biggest Belch in a Bag!

"That gift is a *genius*," I said. "I would love, love, love to buy that thing."

"Who wouldn't?" said Lennie.

"Sí," said José. "Even my grandmother would love a belch in a bag."

Shirley slumped her shoulders.

"I just wish it didn't cost five whole dollars," she said. "Five dollars is a lot of money for a burp."

"Yeah," said Sheldon. "Except for my

grampa, everyone in my family still burps for free."

After that, all of the children walked away to browse some more.

Only not me.

I just kept standing there and standing there.

'Cause the Squeez-a-Burp was the funnest gift I ever heard of.

And I *had* to have one of those things, I tell you!

I just *had* to!

7

Doing the Math

That day, I ran home from my bus stop speedy fast.

'Cause Wednesday is Grampa Miller's day to babysit my baby brother Ollie! And—when I need money—Frank Miller is the man to talk to!

I yelled for him at the top of my voice.

"GRAMPA MILLER! HEY, GRAMPA MILLER! I NEED YOU! I NEED YOU!" I hollered out.

He called up from the basement.

"Junie B.? Is that you? I'm down here

with Ollie! We're fixing the dryer!"

I hurried down there as fast as I could.

Ollie was sitting in the laundry basket. He was hammering his shoe with his red plastic hammer.

I patted him on his head.

Ollie has a screw loose, I think.

After that, I raced to my grampa. And I climbed up on the dryer.

"I am so glad you are here, Grampa Miller! On account of Friday I have to buy gifts at the school gift shop. And Mother is giving me five dollars."

I grabbed him by his shirt collar.

"But I need *more*, Frank! I need five whole dollars more! 'Cause five and five is ten. And ten dollars will buy me everything I want!"

My grampa did a chuckle.

"You sweet little girl. You don't need to spend a lot of money on gifts for Grandma and me," he said. "One dollar apiece is just fine. And I'm sure your mother and daddy and Ollie feel the same way."

He put me down from the dryer.

"It's not how much a gift costs that makes it special, Junie B.," he said. "It's the thought that counts."

I looked and looked at that man.

I was not making myself clear, apparently.

"Okay, here's the deal," I said. "Grampas have to give their grandgirls however much money we want. It's the *rules*."

Grampa Miller raised his eyebrows.

"Oh, it is, is it?" he said.

After that, he chuckled some more. And he went behind the dryer again.

I scratched my head.

This attitude was throwing me for a loop.

I climbed back up on the dryer. And I tapped on his head.

"How come you're not *getting* this, Grampa? It's so simple," I said. "I *need* five dollars and you *have* five dollars. Boom! Do the math."

Grampa Miller looked up at me.

"Boom! Do the math?" he repeated. "Is *that* what you just said?"

Then, all of a sudden, he did a loud hoot of laughing.

"Boom! Do the math! Ha! That's *priceless*!" he said.

I crossed my arms very annoyed.

'Cause *Boom! Do the math* is not a laughing matter.

I got down from the dryer very grouchy.

"Oh, just never mind the whole thing," I grumped.

Then I started to go upstairs. But Grampa called me back.

"Whoa, whoa, whoa. Don't go away mad," he said.

I turned around.

And wait till you hear this!

That man was taking money out of his wallet!

"You're going to do all right in life, little girl," he said real nice.

And then he gave me five whole dollars!

"Thank you, Grampa! Thank you! Thank you!" I said.

Then I gave him my biggest hug ever.

And I ran upstairs to tell Philip Johnny Bob!

Philip Johnny Bob is my bestest stuffed elephant.

I have known him ever since he got manufactured.

I picked him up and threw him in the air.

"THE SQUEEZ-A-BURP, PHILIP! I'M GOING TO GET THE SQUEEZ-A-BURP!" I hollered real joyful.

Philip looked down from the air.

He said to please stop throwing him.

I caught him all safe and sound.

Then I sat him on my pillow. And I told him all about the gift shop. Plus I showed him the list of gift items.

"The gift shop is where you go to buy things for others . . . mostly," I said. "And so I'm only buying one little toy for myself. And that's all. 'Cause one little toy is not even being a shellfish. Right, Phil? Right?"

Right, said Philip. *Plus a good burp is something the whole family can enjoy.*

"Exactly! That's what I think, too!" I said. "Plus everyone will still get their own entire gift that costs a dollar! And so what could be nicer than that?"

You are a giver, said Philip.

I patted him for that nice comment.

Then both of us looked at my list of gifts again. And we read all the stuff that only costs a dollar.

Philip tapped on his trunk. *Hmm. It's hard to choose, isn't it?* he said. *There are some very lovely gift items.*

Then, all of a sudden, Philip's eyes popped right out of his head!

Tattoos!!?? he said. They have tattoos!!??

"Yes, Philip! They have five different kinds of tattoos. And all of them really, really look *real*," I said.

Ooooh, he said. *You can't go wrong with tattoos.*

I clapped very happy.

"I agree!" I said. "And so it is all settled, Philip! I will buy everyone their very own tattoos! And that will use up my whole ten dollars! It works out perfect!"

Me and Philip Johnny Bob did a high five. Then we flopped back on my pillow. And we smiled and smiled.

"Friday is going to be fun!" I said. "'Cause in the morning, I will buy presents! And in the afternoon, Room One will have our Secret Santa party!"

Philip jumped in the air. *Gifts and a Secret Santa party! What can be better than that!*

We flopped back on my pillow again.

Then, all of a sudden, I did a little frown. 'Cause I just remembered something very important.

"Uh-oh," I said.

Uh-oh? asked Philip.

I did a gulp.

"I forgot about the Secret Santa gift, Philip. I have to buy a Secret Santa gift for dumb old May."

Philip shrugged his shoulders.

Yeah? So? he said.

"So all of my ten dollars is already used up," I said. "And so where will I get the money for May?"

Philip looked strange at me. *From Mother and Daddy, of course. Money for school presents is their job, Junie B. Not yours.*

I felt relief in me.

"Whew. Yes. You're right, Phil. It *is* their job," I said. "Plus a gift for May won't even cost much, hardly."

Right, said Philip. *Any dumb old gift will do for May.*

I shook my finger at him.

"Hey, hey, hey. That is not a good attitude, mister," I said.

Then both of us started laughing.

And we couldn't even stop.

8
Being Shellfish

Thursday

Dear first-grade journal,

I cannot believe this situation ~~sitchewashun~~!

Mother said NO MORE MONEY.

Plus Daddy said NO MORE MONEY, too.

They said Grampa Miller already gave me five whole

dollars more! Only HE WAS
NOT ~~SPOSED~~ ^{SUPPOSED} TO TELL THEM
THAT!
   And so GREAT!
   Now I have stress in my
head!
   I NEED AN EXTRA BUCK, I
TELL YOU! I REALLY, REALLY
NEED AN EXTRA BUCK!
                 Your friend,
                 Junie B., First Grader

I closed my journal.

And I looked all around.

My friend Herbert was not writing in his
journal.

I tapped on his head.

"Psst! Herb! I need a buck. I really, really need a buck."

He nodded. "I know, Junie B. You told me that on the bus, remember? But I don't *have* a buck. I really, really don't."

He pulled out his pockets to show me. Then he turned back around.

I tapped on his head again.

"Yeah, only I don't need it *now*, Herb. I need it for *tomorrow*," I explained. "And so just bring me a dollar tomorrow. And I will be your bestest friend."

Herb turned around again.

"You already *are* my bestest friend," he said. "Plus I already *told* you. My mother will only give me the exact amount I need for my gifts. She says every time she gives me extra money, I lose it."

I rolled my eyes.

"*Mothers,*" I said. "They're *all* the same. They think children lose *everything*. And we don't."

Herb nodded. "I know we don't. It's ridiculous."

After that, he came back and looked in my desk.

"Can I borrow a pencil? I lost mine."

I gave him a pencil.

Then I reached across the aisle. And I tapped on Lennie.

"Psst! Lennie! I need an extra buck tomorrow! Can you bring an extra buck? Huh, Lennie? Please, please, please?"

Lennie shook his head. "Sorry, Junie B. But my parents are tightwads. I've never had an extra buck in my life," he said.

José turned around and nodded. "My parents are tightwads, too," he said. "They are *muy tacaños*. That means *tightwads* in Spanish."

Just then, snoopy-head May reached across the row very happy. And she poked me with her pencil.

"Ask me, Junie Jones! Ask me!" she said. "My parents aren't tightwads. I *always* have extra money!"

She reached into her backpack. "I have two whole dollars with me right now! Want to see?"

She took out a shiny plastic wallet.

And wowie wow wow!

There were two whole dollars folded up in there!

"See?" said May. "I *told* you I had money! My parents say I should always have money in case of an emergency."

I sat up very perky.

"Wow. What a coincidence! 'Cause this *is* a 'mergency, May!" I said. "And so if you will just give me one of those dollars, that will take care of my whole entire problem!"

I held out my hand.

But May just frowned her eyebrows.

"Don't be silly. This is for *my* emergencies. Not *yours*, Junie Jones," she said.

She started to put her wallet back.

I talked my fastest.

"But . . . but . . . you are a *giver*, May! Remember that? You are a *giver* . . . and I am a *shellfish*!"

May shrugged. "Yeah? So?"

"So if you *give* me a dollar . . . I will *take* a dollar! And that will make sense for both of us!"

May shook her head.

"No. I can't," she said. "My father says

that friends should never borrow money from each other."

I clapped my hands real thrilled.

"Then it's *perfect*!" I said. "'Cause you and I aren't friends! I don't even *like* you, May! Plus listen to this! I'm not even borrowing the money! You're just giving it to me! And I'm not paying you back!"

May made a mad face at me. Then she

quick put her wallet away again.

I slumped way down in my seat. And I tapped my fingers on my desk.

"I don't get it," I said. "That was the best arguing I ever thought of. What went wrong there?"

Herb turned around.

"I think it might have been the *I don't even like you, May* part," he said.

Lennie nodded. "Plus the *I'm not paying you back* part was probably not the way to go, either."

May leaned her head across the aisle.

"Or else maybe you were never, ever getting the money in the *first* place," she said real mean. "Did you ever think of *that*, Junie Jones?"

I glared my eyes at her.

You're going to be sorry, I thought in my head. *You're really going to be sorry.*

Just then, Mr. Scary stood up at his desk. And he said to put our journals away.

He went to the closet and took out some white paper sacks.

"Boys and girls, these white sacks are going to hold our Secret Santa gifts," he explained. "Today each one of you will decorate your own sack. And tomorrow your Secret Santa will put your gift inside."

He passed them out.

"Please print your name clearly on your sack," he said. "Then at the end of the day, I'll arrange them on the back table. And tomorrow—when we come back from the gift shop—your Secret Santa will go back there and deliver the gift right to your sack! Sound like fun?"

Room One clapped real happy. "Fun!" we said.

"Really, *really* fun!" said May.

She jumped up from her chair.

"Thinking about Secret Santa Day puts me in a happy mood!" she said. "Even Junie Jones can't ruin my Secret Santa Day tomorrow!"

After that, she skipped around her desk. And she sat back down again.

Then I glared at her some more.

Oh, yes, I can, May, I thought again. *I can ruin your day but good.*

I crossed my mad arms.

I would think of a way, no matter what.

I stayed mad at May for the whole rest of the day. 'Cause that meanie girl didn't even *deserve* a Secret Santa gift, I tell you! She didn't deserve any dumb gift at all!

I rode the bus home very grumpity.

"If I was the *real* Santa Claus, I would give May *coal* in her stocking," I grouched to just myself. "That's what she *really* deserves. She deserves *coal.*"

Just then, I sat there very still. And I did not move my muscles.

My brain rewinded itself.

Coal. She deserves coal, it thought again.

Chill bumps came on my arms.

I sat up straighter.

I am a genius, I think.

I zoomed home from my bus stop as fast as a rocket.

Then I ran in my front door . . . and I ran out my back door . . . and I stopped at Daddy's barbecue grill!

The barbecue grill is where Daddy cooks hamburgers and hot dogs. And ha! There is a big bag of coal there!

I reached in my hand.

And I pulled out a lump.

Then I rushed to my room speedy quick. And I showed the coal to Philip Johnny Bob.

"Coal! Coal! I got coal, Phil! See it? Huh? See the coal? Coal is what the *real*

Santa Claus gives mean children. And so that is exactly what I will give May!"

Philip stared at it very curious.

Yeah, only here is the problem. That's not actually coal, he said. *That's called a charcoal briquette.*

I did an annoyed breath at him.

"Yes, Philip. I *know* it's a charcoal briquette," I said. "But I saw a picture of coal before. And it looks exactly like this, kind of. And so May will not even know the difference."

Philip looked at the coal some more. *Oh, I get it,* he said. *The coal is to teach her a lesson. Right?*

"Right, Phil," I said. "That's how come Santa thought of coal in the first place. To teach bad children lessons."

Philip grinned. *Plus after May learns her*

lesson, she can grill herself a hot dog, he said.

I laughed out loud at that funny guy.

He is a joke a minute, I tell you.

I put the coal in a little plastic baggie. And I dropped it in my backpack.

"Ha!" I said. "The perfect Secret Santa gift for meanie May! And it didn't even cost me a single cent!"

I wiped the coal dirt off my hands.

"And that is that. . . . So *there*."

9
The Bestest Gifts

The next morning, Mother gave me a five-dollar bill for the gift shop.

I looked at it in my hand.

"Big whoop," I said.

I would not actually recommend saying that comment.

I got marched to my room for a time-out.

While I was there, I unzipped my back-pack. And I checked on my coal. It was still safe and sound in its plastic baggie.

After that, I got the five dollars Grampa

Miller gave me. And I added it to Mother's money. And I hid all of my dollars in the bottom of my shoe.

Hiding money in your shoe is a good way to keep it safe from pickpocket people.

I saw that on the Travel Channel.

But I must have done something wrong, I think. On account of my dollars got very wadded up at the end of my sock. And they pressed against my little piggy toe.

That's how come—when I got to Room One—I took off my shoe. And I rubbed my toe all better.

May looked over at me. She made a face and held her nose.

"That is disgusting, Junie Jones," she said. "People should not play with their own stinky feet."

I raised my eyebrows very curious.

"Then whose stinky feet should we play with?" I asked.

May put her hands over her ears.

"I am not going to listen to you today," she said. "Today is Secret Santa Day. And I am not going to let you ruin my happy mood."

After that, she turned back around. And she tapped on Lennie's head.

"Happy Secret Santa Day, Lennie! I can't wait for the party. Can you?"

Lennie started to answer. But May interrupted.

"I dressed all in red and green today," she said. "See my socks? One is red and one is green. See?"

Lennie stared at her feet.

"When my grandfather does that, we make him go back and change," he said.

May did a giggle. "But I did it on *pur-pose*, Lennie," she said. "See the ribbons on my braids? One is red and one is green . . . just like my socks. And see? My sweater is green. And my dress is red."

She stood up and turned around.

"This is how everyone should dress on Secret Santa Day!" she said. "Every time I think about our party, it makes my skin prickle. Want to see?"

She closed her eyes for a second.

Then she did a little quiver.

"Woo! I *felt* it!" she said. "I felt my skin prickle again!"

Lennie stared at her.

I stared at her, too.

'Cause I never actually saw her happy before.

"You are acting like a nut," I said.

"How come you are acting like a nut?"

May started to make a mad face. Then, very quick, she smiled again.

"Ha! See that, Junie Jones? See how fast I smiled? Even if you call me names, you still can't ruin my happy mood today."

I made the cuckoo sign at her.

But May kept right on smiling.

Pretty soon, the bell rang to start school.

Mr. Scary took attendance. Also, we did opening ceremonies.

Then hurray, hurray! He said it is time for Room One to go to the gift shop!

I clapped real loud at that happy news.

'Cause pretty soon I would have my very own Squeez-a-Burp! And that is a dream come true!

I sprang out of my chair. And I ran to the door.

"Yay! Yay! Yay! I'm first in line! I'm first in line!" I called real joyful.

Then I jumped up and down. And I twirled all around. Plus also, I skipped to and fro.

Mr. Scary said to *please settle down*.

But my feet would *not* stop bouncing!

That's how come Mr. Scary finally gave up on me. And he held my hand. And both of us led Room One to the gift shop!

I zoomed in the door as fast as I could.

Then I ran straight to Table Five.

But wait till you hear this!

There was only *one* Squeez-a-Burp left!

I did a gasp at that situation.

Then I quick grabbed it!

And I hid it in my sweater.

And I zoomed to the gift-shop lady speedy fast.

"Quick! Hurry! Put it in a bag," I whispered. "I don't want people to see me buying this. Or they might call me a shellfish."

The gift lady looked odd at me.

Then I handed her my money.

And she put the burp in a bag.

And no one even saw!

I hid the bag in my sweater pocket.

Then I walked real calm to Table One. And I picked out five sets of tattoos.

And guess what?

Everyone in my family got their own special kind! 'Cause Grampa Miller got dinosaurs. And Mother got dragons. And Daddy got pirates. And Ollie got kitty cats. And my grandma Helen Miller got the nice variety of swamp animals.

"She will love these things," I said. "There's a swamp animal to match every occasion."

After that, I skipped to the gift lady. And I gave her the rest of my money.

She put them in my same bag.

I smiled when I looked in there.

"These are the bestest gifts I ever bought," I told her.

The gift lady nodded. "Yes," she said. "Tattoos and a belch. Your family will be delighted."

I did a happy giggle.

Then I ran to the door of the gift shop. And I lined up to go back to Room One.

"I'm all done, people! I'm all done with my shopping!" I called out.

May walked by me. "This isn't a *race,* Junie Jones," she said.

I made a face at her. Then I sat down on the floor. And I waited and waited and waited.

Room One is the slowest shoppers you ever saw.

Then . . . *finally* . . . Mr. Scary said it is time to go back to our room. And so everyone lined up behind me. And I led them back.

All of us were buzzing very much. 'Cause after lunch would come the party, of course! And the party meant HA! WE GET OUR SECRET SANTA GIFTS!

Mr. Scary hurried to the back of the room.

"Boys and girls, all of the paper sacks you decorated yesterday are lined up here on the back table," he said. "When I call your name, you will walk back here, and I'll help you find the right bag, okay? Then you'll secretly drop your Secret Santa gift inside and walk back to your desk."

He smiled. "We don't have much time. So we've got to be orderly," he said. "The rest of you will stay busy writing or drawing in your journals. And remember . . . no peeking!"

He called Lucille's name first.

She skipped to the front of the room. And did a twirl.

"This is just in case anyone missed seeing my expensive party dress today," she said.

Then she skipped to the back of the room with her gift-shop bag.

I looked over at May. She was getting out her journal and not paying attention to me.

Very sneaky, I reached my hand in my backpack. And I pulled out the baggie with her coal inside.

Then I bent over very secret—and I dropped the coal in my gift-shop bag.

The plastic made a crinkle sound.

May turned her head to see.

I smiled.

She was too late.

The coal was ready to go.

10
Pressure

Friday

Dear first-grade journal,

I keep thinking about May's present.

I wonder what will happen when she sees the coal?

I wonder what her face will look like?

I wonder if she will learn a lesson?

I wonder if Santa will be proud of me?

That is all the things I am wondering.

Your friend,
Junie B., First Grader

Just then, I felt a poke.

It was May.

"Are you getting excited, Junie Jones? *I'm* getting excited," she said.

Lennie heard her.

"Me too," he said. "I'm getting excited, too."

Herb and José both nodded their heads.

"Me too," they said together.

May squirmed and bounced around in her seat.

She was acting like a regular kid.

"Having a Secret Santa makes you feel like you have a best friend," she said very giggling. "Right, Lennie? Huh? It makes you feel like you have a best friend, doesn't it?"

Lennie looked funny at her.

"But I *do* have a best friend, May," he said. "My best friend is José."

José smiled. "Back at'cha, Len," he said.

Herb pointed at me. "And my best friend is Junie B.," he said.

I poked him very fun. "And *my* bestest friend is y-o-u, Herbert!"

Just then, May stopped bouncing and squirming. And her face lost all its happy.

"Oh," she said real soft. "Right."

Her shoulders slumped a little bit.

"Well, anyway . . . that's what it makes

me feel like," she said. "Having a Secret Santa makes me feel like *I* have a best friend, too."

After that, all of us sat there very still.

The mood did not feel happy anymore.

Very slow, Lennie and José turned back around in their chairs.

Me and Herb turned around, too.

We didn't talk again. We just sat there and waited for Mr. Scary to call our names.

Finally, he called José . . . and then Lennie.

May started to get excited again.

I heard her whispering to herself. "It's almost my turn! It's almost my turn! It's almost my turn!"

Just then, Lennie came back from the gift table. And May sprang right up.

"Me! Me! It's time for me!" she hollered.

Then she grabbed her gift bag. And she ran right back to Mr. Scary.

Pretty soon, it would be my turn, too.

I picked up my gift-shop bag, and I peeked at the coal.

My stomach felt a little bit sickish at the sight of it.

I wonder if Santa's stomach feels sickish before he gives children coal?

May skipped back to her chair. And she started singing "Frosty the Snowman."

I closed my ears. And I tried not to hear her being happy.

Finally, Mr. Scary called my name.

"Junie B.?" he said.

My heart pounded real hard.

I picked up my gift bag and walked to the back table.

Mr. Scary winked at me.

"Do you need any help?" he asked.

I shook my head real fast. "No," I said. "No help! No, thank you. No help, Mr. Scary. I can do this all by myself."

My hands felt sweatish and clammish.

I wiped them on my skirt.

Then I waited very patient for my teacher to walk away.

After he was gone, I picked up May's gift sack. And I held it in my hand.

It was the beautifulest sack on the table.

It was covered with shiny gold stars and sparkly red glitter. Plus also, there were beautiful green bows all over the sides.

I did a gulp.

I wondered how it would look with the black coal inside it.

I wondered if May would be sad when she saw it.

I did another gulp.

I wondered if she would stop singing "Frosty."

Just then, I heard my name again.

"Junie B.?" said Mr. Scary. "Are you sure you don't need any help back there?"

Then oh no! Oh no!

Before I could even answer, I heard his feet!

He was coming back to help me!

I felt pressure in my head.

There was no time left!

And so, boom!

I did it!

I grabbed May's present out of my gift bag! And I dropped it right in her sack!

Then I hurried back to my desk speedy fast. And I plopped down in my seat.

I took some deep breaths.

It was *over.*

And *that* was *that.*

The end.

11

May's Big Surprise

Room One went to lunch.

I did not eat my sandwich.

Also, I did not eat my carrot sticks.

'Cause how can I even swallow stuff when my stomach still feels sickish?

I kept thinking and thinking about what I did.

Only it didn't even matter anymore.

'Cause now it was too late.

After we got back from lunch, Mr. Scary put on a Santa hat. And he passed out cake and cookies and punch. Plus also, he gave everyone a candy cane.

After that, he went back to our gift sacks. And he folded their tops shut.

"Okay, everyone! This is the moment we've all been waiting for! Ready for me to deliver the Secret Santa gifts?" he said.

"READY!" hollered Room One.

Mr. Scary smiled. "When I give you your gift sack, please keep it on your desk," he said. "Then—when everyone has their sack—we will open them all together."

May jumped up and clapped.

"That is a deal, mister!" she said real silly.

Then she sat back down.

And she sang "Frosty" some more.

And all of Room One started singing with her!

Except not me.

Because I still did not feel cheery about what I did. And there was nothing I could even do about it.

Pretty soon, Mr. Scary handed May her sack.

She stood up and skipped around her desk again. She was still belting out "Frosty."

I drummed my fingers on my desk.

"Okay, now her joy is actually getting on my nerves," I said to just myself.

Finally, Mr. Scary gave me my gift sack, too.

"Thank you," I said.

Only I didn't actually feel that happy. 'Cause May's gift kept staying on my mind.

As soon as all the sacks were passed out, Mr. Scary walked to the front of the room. And he beamed real big.

"Okay, everyone! When I count to three, we'll open our gifts. Ready?" he said.

"READY!" we shouted.

Mr. Scary started to count.

"One . . . two . . . three!"

Then *whoosh!*

All of the children pulled out their gifts at once.

Except not me, again.

And not May.

Instead, she just stared into her sack. And she sat there real frozen.

Her face had shock on it.

Lennie turned around to see what she got.

But May didn't move.

"What did you get, May?" he asked. "What's wrong? Huh? What's wrong?"

May didn't answer.

Then José turned around, too. And so did Herb. And Sheldon. And Shirley.

"What's wrong with May?" they said. "Is something wrong with May?"

May kept staying frozen.

Finally, Mr. Scary came back to her desk. And he bent down next to her.

"May? Is there a problem?" he asked real quiet.

May did a big swallow. Her eyes had a little bit of tears in them, I think.

Then, very slow, she handed him the gift sack. And he looked inside.

His mouth dropped open at that sight.

"Oh," he said. "Oh my."

He gave it back.

May looked up at him. "I can't believe anybody would *do* this," she said real soft.

"Do what, May?" asked Sheldon.

May breathed real deep.

Then she reached into her bag. And she pulled out her gift.

Everyone gasped real loud.

They could not believe their eyeballs, I tell you!

They waited to get their breath back.

Then everybody started shouting all at once.

"THE SQUEEZ-A-BURP! THE SQUEEZ-A-BURP! SOMEONE GOT MAY THE SQUEEZ-A-BURP!"

"That thing costs a *fortune*!" called Shirley.

"Squeeze it!" yelled Sheldon.

"Yes! Squeeze it!" yelled the children.

May started to grin.

Then she stood up kind of slow. And she gave that thing a squeeze.

And HA!

It burped beautifully!

Room One laughed their heads off.

"Do it again! Do it again! Do it again!"
they shouted.

And so May burped again.

And Room One laughed again.

And they kept going on and on like that.

Finally, May sat down for a second. And she fanned herself with her hand.

"I think I'm being *popular*," she said very stunned.

Then she quick stood up again. And she skipped around the room. And she kept on squeezing her burp.

It felt happy to watch her, sort of.

Also, it felt hard.

'Cause I really, *really* wanted that toy, that's why. I wanted it *real* bad.

Only it didn't even belong to me now.

And it never, ever would.

My gift sack was still sitting on my desk.

I put it on my lap and looked inside.

"Crayons!" I said very surprised. "My Secret Santa bought me brand-new crayons! Who even knew that I needed these things!"

All of Room One turned around at once.

"Everyone," they said.

I opened the box and breathed their new-crayon smell.

Then I lined them up on my desk. And I smiled real happy.

'Cause greenie was not a stubbie!

And my red's head was perfectly pointy!

I smiled even bigger.

Then I drank some punch and ate a cookie.

My stomach felt better now.

Pretty soon, May skipped back to her desk. And she fanned herself again.

"Whew! Being popular really gets you tired," she said. "Right, Junie Jones? Right?"

I looked back and nodded.

"Right," I said kind of quiet.

After that, May sat down. And both of us ate our cake. And we licked our candy canes.

It was very peaceful of us.

We were having goodwill, I believe.

After May finished, she wiped off her mouth with her napkin.

"Well, I'd better get back to my skipping now," she said. "I have a lot more burping to do before the bell rings."

She jumped up from her chair.

But instead of skipping away, she just stood there with the Squeez-a-Burp. And she smiled at me.

Then, all of a sudden, she reached across the aisle. And she put it on my desk.

"Want to try it, Junie Jones?" she said. "Want to do a burp?"

I raised my eyebrows very shocked.

"Really, May? No kidding? You would really, really let me do that?"

Then—before she could change her mind—I quick picked it up. And I squeezed that thing as loud as I could.

And WOWIE WOW WOW!

It was the biggest burp of the day!

May clapped and clapped.

"Ha! That was a *good* one, Junie B.!" she said. "You did *good*!"

The words floated inside my head.

I smiled.

I did good.

After that, May picked up her toy. And she started to skip away.

Then—WHOA! HOLD THE PHONE!

It hit me like a brick!

I jumped up, and I grabbed May's arm.

"Wait a second, May! Did you just say my B.?" I asked. "'Cause I really, really thought you said my B. just now! I'm almost positive you did, in fact!"

May tapped on her chin.

"Hmm. Really?" she asked. "I said your B.? That's funny."

Then she did a little smile. And she skipped away.

I sat there a second.

Then my whole face got happy. Only I don't even know why. 'Cause I *still* really wanted that Squeez-a-Burp, I tell you! And so how come I felt so good inside?

Maybe—when I got home from school—Philip Johnny Bob would help me figure it out.

But for right now, there was only one thing I was really, really hoping for.

I picked up my new black crayon. And I opened my journal.

Dear Santa,
    I really hope that you

were watching me just now.
   That's all I hope.
       Love,
                    Giver
       Junie B., ~~First Grader~~
P.S. You don't happen to have
an extra Squeez-a-Burp up
there, do you?

   PEACE
~~PEECE~~ AND GOODWILL.
       Amen.

118

Laugh yourself silly with

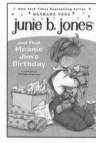

ALL the Junie B. Jones books!

 Junie B. Jones Is a Graduation Girl

 Junie B. Jones First Grader (at last!)

 Junie B. Jones Boss of Lunch

 Junie B. Jones Toothless Wonder

 Junie B. Jones Cheater Pants

 Junie B. Jones One-Man Band

 Junie B. Jones Shipwrecked

 Junie B. Jones Boo... and I MEAN It!

 Junie B. Jones Jingle Bells, Batman Smells! (P.S. So Does May.)

 Junie B. Jones Aloha-ha-ha!

 Junie B. Jones Dumb Bunny

 Junie B. Jones Turkeys We Have Loved and Eaten (and Other Thankful Stuff)

 Junie B. Jones Top-Secret Personal Beeswax: A Journal by Junie B. (and me!)

 Junie B.'s Essential Survival Guide to School

 Junie B. Jones These Puzzles Hurt My Brain! Book

 Junie B. My Valentime

Don't miss this next book about my fun in first grade!

Junie B. and her family are going on a vacation to Hawaii! Will the trip be picture-perfect? Or will it be Aloha-*horrible*?

Available Now!